'Christmas Miracle' Is Just A Saying

Amy Laurens

Other Works

Find other works by the author at
www.amylaurens.com/books

'CHRISTMAS MIRACLE' IS JUST A SAYING

Amy Laurens

AUSTRALIA

Print ISBN: 978-1-922434-93-7
eBook ISBN: 9798224771097

www.inkprintpress.com

National Library of Australia Cataloguing-in-Publication Data
Laurens, Amy 1985—
Christmas Miracle Is Just A Saying
64 p.   cm.
ISBN: 978-1-922434-93-7
Inkprint Press, Canberra, Australia
1. Fiction—Fantasy—Urban 2. Fiction—Fantasy—Paranormal

Summary: Arabella's Christmas Eve out on the town turns to disaster when her best friend, Jenson the wereshark, is attacked down at the beach.

First Edition: November 2024

Cover design © Inkprint Press
Shark line art © s4rt4 via Deposit Photos

PLEASE NOTE: This cover has been designed using AI-generated stock art via Canva's Magic Media app and Adobe Photoshop.

This book was written and published on Ngunnawal country. The author would like to acknowledge the people who have told their stories here for countless generations.

With thanks to Clare, Liana, Dean and Shaun, all
of whom made suggestions that made this a much,
much better book.

'Christmas Miracle' Is Just A Saying

ANYONE WHO SAYS THEY LIKE CHRISTMAS IS LYING. That's my default position, anyway, because honestly, all it means is dealing with family secrets and fights, guilt and gifts equally unwanted, misery wrapped up in a giant glistening bow.

Okay, okay, the lights are pretty and the music isn't entirely questionable, and it's kind of cool that the whole city is, like, vibing together for the most part, night-time streets lined with sweaty bodies trying to cool down after the heat of the summer day and vibrant cocktails brighter than tinsel and the women's dresses and yes, the lights I mentioned, strings of them, cobwebbing from trunk to pale trunk to canvas restaurant awning down the street... Yeah, okay, fine. I like the time of year.

I just hate everything else that comes with it.

Which is why, when my phone buzzed in my bra for the third time in as many minutes, I ignored it. Not hard, honestly; the noise of the city street party made regular conversation impossible, the crowd ebbing and flowing, swelling and shushing like the ocean that lay only two blocks over, itself a background susurrus that added to the sense of urgency in the air: it's coming, it's coming, it's coming.

I inhaled the salt wind deeply, tongue-tip dabbing a drop of some tropical-flavoured liquid that purported to be non-alcoholic but was making me suspiciously buzzy away from the corner of my mouth.

Jenson jostled me from the right, himself being elbowed aside to make way for a tall bear of a man in a suit that looked far too sharp, too polished for this particular street, even in the dark.

"You right?" I murmured to a tousled-haired Jenson, manoeuvring the cup of suspicious liquid out of harm's way with one hand and digging my phone out of my bra with the other.

He muttered something in reply, too low for me to hear, and definitely too low for the bear-man to hear—but the bear-man turned anyway, pinning Jenson to the spot for a heart-stopping moment as the sea of bodies swayed through the street around us. Something about him seemed to shimmer for a moment, an aquamarine sheen over his form in the crowded night.

Eh. Probably part of some elaborate Christmas Eve costume or something. I wiped sweat from my forehead with the back of my arm and thumbed my phone unlocked.

Jenson vibrated beside me, tension and pugilism and pent-up aggression.

I rolled my eyes as the bear-like man with his thick, short beard and light-brown curls responded in kind, and turned my attention back to my phone. Whatever. Jenson was a big boy. He could look after himself.

Urgh. The phone call had been Mum. Again.

"He shouldn't be here," Jenson muttered, hands balling at his sides.

I glanced at the packed street that was currently exploding with Christmas Eve frivolity as people shopped and strolled and clustered out the front of White Rabbit for its annual free party. Conversations and laughter washed over us to the pumping party bassline, some amped-up version of a Christmas carol I could *almost* recognise through the noise. "Why not? Everyone else on the planet is."

"He's fey."

Ice clutched my chest for just an instant—then I worked my tongue against the inside of my cheek, the taste all fruity and sour from the punch, and shoved the phone back in my bra. "Let's get out of here," I said, catching Jenson by a skinny wrist and pulling him around. "I'm sick of this place."

BearMan was not fey. No fey would be that stupid. Jenson was just jumpy in the crowd and spooking at shadows. I shouldn't have dragged him here to begin with. Crowds were never his favourite.

Jenson's body stayed tense a moment longer, resistant to my hand—then he broke off and relaxed into an easy stride beside me. He straightened his black-rimmed glasses. Harrumphed.

"Yeah, yeah," I said, rolling my eyes—and my shoulders. "You could have taken him, I know, I know."

"It's not that." Jenson cut through the crowd like the shark he was, late-night last-minute shoppers and public party-goers avoiding him alike. Walking with him was always like that, like regular people could sense that something was off about him and it made them nervous. Even in the semi-light of the Christmas lanterns and street lamps, I could see the little glances people were giving him, and all he was doing was walking.

"No?" I said, tugging on his arm to both slow him down and steer him sideways so the oncoming mother-with-pram wouldn't need to divert around him. A waft of something hot and sugary hit me.

Jenson muttered something inaudible over the vibrating chatter of the crowd.

I rolled my eyes skyward, a vague blackness somewhere up there above the street sparkle. *Heaven help me and give me patience.* I tugged at his arm again, hard.

There was only one solution when he got like this. "That's it," I said. "We're going for a swim."

That slowed him down.

Stopped him right in his tracks, actually.

"Jen." I skip-hopped sideways into the road as a gaggle of white twenty-something males sauntered down the footpath. (Didn't matter, the road had been closed to traffic since five.) "This is non-negotiable. You're jumpier than a toad tonight and it's ruining my chill. I'm taking you for a swim, and then we are going to spend the rest of the night partying like it's Christmas Eve and we have no family to bother us, okay? Beach or boardwalk?"

He stood, skinny frame rigid like a clothes rack under his baggy tee, fingers knotting and flexing at his sides.

My bra buzzed again.

Summoning every ounce of maturity I had, I left it alone instead of hurling it across the street.

"Fine." I turned on my heel, letting the crowd wash over me, someone's rosy perfume curling through my hair, sweat and heat and salt a hot summer bouquet. "I'll go by myself."

...Three, four...

I pressed my lips tightly together to hide the satisfied smile as Jenson appeared at my shoulder, a little knot of blackhole energy.

"Beach," he grunted.

I nodded, and pressed a hand against my chest as my phone buzzed yet-a-freaking-gain.

THE BEACH WAS SHOCKINGLY EMPTY AFTER THE PRESS AND hustle of the party street, the ocean drowning out the noise of the people now several blocks away with its shush and sliiiide, shush and sliiiide. The city lights reflected off the ocean back where we'd come from, golden and shimmery. Saltwater-air curled around me, fresh and cool and mellow. I inhaled deeply, letting the humid air fill me.

Walking in shoes on sand was for punks, so I'd removed my ballet flats and had them casually slung in one hand with Jenson's glasses, and was enjoying the feel of the cold, wet sand scratching between my toes. I'd hated that feeling for so long. I'd grown up in the mountains, and beaches were something that Happened to Other People. I'd always found them glarey, gritty, crowded places that were either blisteringly hot on the sand or butt-freezingly cold in the water.

It had taken a few years for Jenson to bring me around, and visiting at weird times like the middle of winter or the dark of night did a lot to dispel my initial reluctance.

I still wasn't dumb enough to swim in the dark, though. So I wandered up and down my claimed stretch of sand to the soundtrack of the waves, counting the few stars bright enough to outshine the city lights, watching boats come in and out of the bay, their red and green navigational lights like little Christmas fairies out there in the dark.

Huh. That was an old-me association. New-me knew that fairies weren't little, wouldn't be caught dead skimming the water's surface like that—at least not around here—and that they mostly glowed blue or gold.

Also most of them hated Christmas almost as much as I did, though for more cultural reasons. I suppose when you're considered an unwanted third race by most of the people celebrating the Christmas season (religiously or otherwise) you're bound be a bit bitter about it.

Light flashed on the horizon: a deep summer storm rolling in with the tide.

I shivered, and not from the wind that was picking up—it was still warm, though it was whipping the tops off the waves in drifts of white foam that no doubt would still be cold.

But it had been a while since I'd witnessed a storm out over the ocean like this, and even if it had been totally mundane I still would have quivered with anticipation, the thrill of it rising in my chest and propelling my breath along.

This storm, though? Anything but mundane. As the lightning flashed again it lit the sky up in tones of red and magenta and violet.

The hair on my arms prickled; it wasn't just electrical energy charging the air.

I pressed my free hand against the nerves trilling in my belly, the silky fabric of my best red Christmas dress cool in the night air. Hopefully Jenson wouldn't be too long. Magical storms weren't common—I'd only seen a couple before— but the energy they held was immense, and I didn't relish the idea of being stuck out in one.

BearMan had rattled him good though, and he might be k's away by now, skimming deep down along dark sandy depths where direction was measured in currents and temperature, and food by electrical pulses.

I shivered again and pushed the image of the scary dark deep away. It was one thing learning to enjoy a bit of a bob in a clear, calm sea where the scariest thing around was my highly-motived-to-make-sure-I-stayed-safe friend.

I'd followed him out deeper once.

He'd forgotten about me. Distracted by the lure of the open water.

If you've never had a panic attack a k offshore, I don't recommend it. Just in case you were wondering. I'd spent two nights in the hospital for drowning even after Jenson had come to his senses and dragged me back to shore. I still had the scar on my right hand where he'd caught at me with his teeth.

Lightning flickered again, closer now, forking across half the sky, regular silver-gold, then crimson, fuchsia, lilac.

My phone buzzed again.

I plucked at the wisps of hair that the wind was plastering to my mouth, dug my phone out of my bra, and swiped to answer. "Hi, Mum," I said, failing at keeping the exasperation from my tone. I'd mostly quit talking to her the same time she'd quit talking to Dad, but hell if she wasn't being persistent tonight.

More lightning, closer still, close enough that it lit up the sky—and the sea.

Wow the storm was moving fast.

"Arabella, where the *fuck* are you?"

Something in the shallows, a movement under the crystalline waves that caught my eye for just an instant.

Big. Too big for Jenson?

Something queasy slithered in my stomach.

"Sorry Mum, gotta go." I hung up, pushing hair back from my face in the wind, scanning the waves that were whipping up to a frenzy.

A huge splash, out beyond the breakers, practically a geyser as something breached the surface. Lightning flashed and the column of water lit up, red and angry.

Something was out there.

Something that wasn't Jenson.

"Come on, come on," I muttered. Jen *could* be far away by now… but something told me that was unlikely. Whatever that thing was out there, Jen would know about it—and he'd come right back to tell me, I was sure.

Another gigantic splash, this time lit purple. Frantic flailing on the surface, still out beyond the waves.

My heart pounded. I licked at salty lips, pushing my hair back again, impatient with it.

Thunder cracked.

Something surfaced between sets of white-tipped waves, barely visible in the poor light.

Lightning.

It was an arm, flung high, flailing for help.

No lifeguards here, that was certain.

I tucked the phone back into my bra, left my ballet flats and J's glasses in the sand, and waded out into cold-but-not-freezing water.

Splash, step, splash, step… A wave shushed in and slopped up my waist. "Jenson you bastard," I muttered at the night as I tensed with cold, my heart hammering loud enough I could hear it over the waves, "this dress was far too expensive for this." Should have left it on the sand.

Lightning. A sharp crack of thunder.

I jumped.

Another wave caught me, this time sloshing up my chest. I scraped hair away from my mouth, spat out salt water, fought for balance in the shifting sand below my feet.

Should have left the phone on the sand too. I took it out and held it over my head as though that might keep it drier, waiting for the next lightning flash to illuminate the water. I couldn't go any deeper. With the storm lashing the waves, I'd be swept right out to sea.

"C'mon Jen, where are you…"

A heaving splash not four steps in front of me as something monstrous broke through the surf.

Cold spray soaked my head and shoulders. My pulse stuttered—and I recognised the awkward, nightmarish shape of Jenson mid-shift.

I lunged at him with just enough presence of mind to shove my phone back in my bra, catching at his substantial weight as adrenaline crashed over me like one of the waves currently trying to drown us. "Jen! Jen, are you okay, are you okay?"

Salt water dripped down my face, slicked my lips. I wiped it away, impatient.

Adrenaline pulsing through me, the crash of the waves, thunder above us. Jenson's horrific shape contorted, throwing me off balance as an anguished groan tore from him.

Lightning.

Nearly human.

I dragged him closer to the beach

Thunder.

Nearly human.

Almost there.

"Hang on, Jen." I snatched at him as he flailed and nearly fell, and then it was all limbs and salty waves stinging my eyes and his fingers digging tightly into my upper arm as he wailed and there was something dark on his face, his neck. I wiped at it.

Lighting.

Fully human.

Bleeding. Maybe bleeding bad.

We stumbled up onto shore, collapsed on the wet sand where the waves still grabbed and caught at our feet.

Please still work, please still work. I shook the water off my phone, shouldered hair out of my face, winced as lightning and thunder hit as one.

Switched on my phone's torch.

Found the source of the blood.

His neck.

My gut clenched.

I went rigid with shock, with horror.

Jenson writhed on the sand, back arching, hands scrabbling.

Oh God.

Oh God oh God.

Something had taken a bite out of his neck.

THE ANGRY BUZZ OF MY PHONE JOLTED ME TO MY SENSES.

"Mum," I snapped, "I need to call an ambulance."

"*No.* Listen to me."

I froze, shallow breaths caught in my throat, the sky shattering red and pink and purple above me, my best friend writhing on the sand as blood pumped a dark stain beneath him. The wind was cold now I was wet.

But Mum's tone cut through all that.

"What's going on?" I whispered, fingers biting into the edge of the phone.

"Tell me where you are."

I did.

"Don't move. Apply pressure. Someone will be there in two minutes." She hung up.

I stared at the phone screen for a moment, until a sharp thundercrack made me jump.

Shit.

Jenson.

Pressure.

I grappled with the skirt of my dress—stupid synthetic fabrics not designed to tear.

The phone went down in the sand, the torchlight casting bizarre shadows over Jenson as he lay gasping.

The writhing had stopped. That had to be a bad sign.

I yanked the dress's side zip down and struggled out of the red fabric that was a lot more clingy and skin-tight now it was wet.

Crouched on the sand in bra and undies, I pressed the dress to Jenson's neck and shivered in the wind.

So much blood. I could smell it, metallic and sweet—no, there was no way I could smell it, my nose wasn't that good and the air was all saltwater and storm. I gasped an inhale. Must be imagining it, dredging it up from old memories, and—

A hissing noise.

I cast around, heart pounding wildly. What in the world...?

But the mysterious noise resolved itself a moment later: rain, spitting furiously down on the ocean and, a bare second after that, the beach, and Jenson—and me. I shivered again, my hair plastered to my face, one hand bracing the other side of Jenson's neck as I pressed with everything I had against the wound.

Lightning-thunder.

My throat hurt.

Right. I was crying.

Instinctively, I wiped my face against my shoulder—but there was no point, the rain was pelting now, a rushing roar over the growling rage of the surf.

Jenson caught my arm.

I couldn't make out his face—I had no hand free to hold the phone and the torch was mostly illuminating the rain as it sluiced through the air—but it seemed like he was looking at me. "It's okay," I said, and my voice came out raspy, barely audible over the storm.

Lightning flashed. Thunder.

He *was* looking at me, eyes wide, frightened. His grip on my arm tightened.

I squeezed back with the hand bracing the crook of his neck.

Another lightning/thunder duo: down the beach someone tall was hustling toward us. My pulse skipped. The help Mum had sent. No one else would be dumb enough to be out here.

The tall someone drew closer.

I sat up a little straighter as another flash of lightning illuminated his face.

In all the whole wide world, I would never have expected it to be BearMan, crouching down at Jenson's other side, now mostly obscured by a light raincoat but with a slice of my phone's torchlight crossing his heavily-bearded face.

"What?" My brain stuttered to a halt.

"Pressure," the man snapped, a gruff kind of shout over the noise of the rain, the waves, the thunder—my heartbeat.

I gave my head a shake and firmed up the pressure on Jenson's neck. "What are you doing here?" I semi-shouted.

"Your mum sent me."

...The actual?? "Why?"

He frowned deeply, eyebrows knotting. "To help." He gestured at Jenson, something indistinct gripped in both his hands.

"What?"

He raised whatever it was, suspending it over Jenson's chest. "Call it an early Christmas miracle," he shouted.

The globe—tennis-sized—began to glow with rainbow iridescence in the night, a ball of warm light gilding the rain that fell now like Christmas glitter.

Cold, wet Christmas glitter, but I always said Christmas was miserable, right?

BearMan released the globe gently; it hung in the storm about a foot above Jenson's chest.

I froze—and not because the rain cascading over my nearly-naked body was cold.

Iridescent light.

Iridescent light.

My eyes widened.

BearMan nodded, a quick bow of the chin in acknowledgement—and for the briefest of instants, his eyes glowed aquamarine.

"You *are* a—"

He winced, and I swallowed the word they hated. Not that any of the euphemisms seemed appropriate, not here, not up close and personal.

Jenson groaned.

Right. Pressure—

He was writhing again, but this time the gradual re-energising wriggle of someone fading back into life with each flash of lightning.

I let my ruined red dress fall away—and shuddered at the way the skin around his wound was crawling in the shifting, iridescent light of the sphere, rippling and edging back together.

He drew in a deep, shuddering breath—and whipped his head around, scowling furiously as BearMan shifted in the sand. "What did you to do me?" His voice was weak, but the horror was evident.

I puffed up my cheeks and let the air out slowly. Hoo boy. This was *not* going to be pretty.

I rolled my shoulders, remembered I was in nothing but skin-soaked bra and panties, and stood up, taking a half step back to let the darkness obscure at least a little of my near-nakedness— and to give the boys some space.

I grabbed up my phone, thumbed it unlocked, and switched off the torch. BearMan's magical glow-ball was doing a better job of providing ambience anyway.

Which—I tilted my head—BearMan was doing a good job of ignoring Jenson's attempt to pick a fight—

Oh, nope, okay, he'd just been zoning out finishing his magic or something, because now he was getting up abruptly, snatching the globe out of the air and whirling away, and Jenson was obviously feeling better because he was leaping to his feet after the f—the BearMan, and pursuing him down the storm-swept beach in a manner highly reminiscent of a tiny peewee bird haranguing an eagle.

I snorted.

I sighed.

And I trudged down the beach after them. Jenson's clothes would no doubt be soaked where we'd left them at the edge of the sand, but he had another thing coming if he didn't think I'd be stealing his t-shirt regardless.

 city streets without either of them killing the other. The storm even slacked, continuing its race inland, taking the thunder and lightning and heavy rain with it, leaving only a warm drizzle that was, by contrast, quite pleasant.

Less good news: Once I'd caught up and struggled into Jenson's soaked t-shirt—large enough to imitate a loose, wet mini-dress—BearMan informed us in no uncertain terms that a) the healing he'd done on Jenson was temporary, and b) we would therefore need to hightail it somewhere safe so he could make the solution more permanent asap.

I'd agreed—until he'd revealed where we were going. "No," I said as we cut through the brightly lit car park, packed with late-night last-minute shoppers. "*Hell* no. Over my dead body."

"Over his dead body." BearMan tilted his eyebrows at Jenson and clambered nonchalantly into a silver sedan, streetlights glinting off its paintwork.

I was not going to punch the car. It wouldn't help, and it would hurt my knuckles. So no: no punching.

I breathed the salt-and-ozone air deeply instead as the dial tone on the car phone rang, clearly audible through the car's closed doors in the annoying manner of vehicles everywhere.

"What do we do?" Jenson murmured.

A woman pushing an overloaded shopping trolley strode past, footsteps crunching in the wet gravel, the trolley clunk-clunk-kerclunking along.

I shoved my soaked, now-dark hair out of my face. "That's—"

My phone buzzed. I looked down and answered on autopilot.

Mum said, "Get in the car," and hung up.

Of course she did.

I snapped my mouth shut with a click, shoved the phone forcefully back in my bra, climbed into the car, and slammed the door.

Fine.

Fine.

Just peachy effing fine.

Jenson slid into the backseat from the other side. "I guess we're going then."

I snorted. Ignored the look BearMan gave me in the rearview. Studied the carpark full of the usual blue and red and white and silver vehicles, skulking under the streetlights.

Stupid late-night shoppers with their obsession over Christmas gifts. Stupid twinkle lights, glaring off the cars and making me squint. Stupid rain, spattering against the car window and glittering under the orange streetlights. The whole thing was even worse as we picked up speed on the street, rain and twinkle lights and wet-road reflections blurring into one great, giant glitter ball.

Stuck in a glitter ball on Christmas Eve, chauffeured on a direct route to my mother's.

I told you I hate Christmas.

IT DIDN'T HELP, OF COURSE, THAT I HADN'T BEEN HOME FOR about two years. Well, more than two years, I'd definitely missed the last two Christmases and not a single person nor anything they could say would make me regret it. I did *not* need a repeat of the year before that, the one where Mum had had a go at me for hanging out with Jenson, telling me he was going to get me into "all kinds of trouble I didn't even know existed"—all while Jenson sat red-faced at the dinner table, trying to pretend like he'd gone temporarily deaf as he chased minted peas around his plate with a knife and fork.

Not to mention that had been the last Christmas with Dad.

I sighed deeply and leaned my forehead against the cool glass of the car's backseat window. "You know it takes like fifteen kinds of toxic chemicals to recreate that new-car smell, right?"

BearMan snorted. "Doesn't stink worse than any other fake scent you humans have invented."

I opened my mouth, and completely failed to think of a witty comeback.

Fuck, hey.

The big guy was a fairy. The *other* f-word.

I snorted at my hilarity—and it changed abruptly to another sigh as we pulled into the driveway of my mother's house. The weathered little one-storey had seen better days if I was going to be honest—which Mum always was, so why let an opportunity pass. She'd lined the gutters with red and gold Christmas lights, and two twinkling reindeer stood in the front yard—pretty, until you saw the patchy, scraggly grass they were illuminating in the dark.

The storm had rolled past and the air smelled crisp and clean, with stars above mimicking the lights on the house, albeit in a less competitive way.

BearMan got out and closed his door with a thunk.

Jenson cast me a long look then did the same.

The glass of the window was pleasantly cool against my forehead. And it was quiet in here, especially now. And I didn't have to answer any questions in here, and I didn't have to lie to anyone in here, and I didn't have to feel guilty that I'd barely spoken to my parents or sisters in over two years in here.

The door popped open and I overbalanced, caught by my seatbelt and my arm against the driver's headrest.

"Thought I might find you here."

"Hey, Dad," I said, giving the tall, dark man now blocking my view of most of the stars a puzzled look. "What are you doing here?"

"If you answered your phone once in a while, kiddo, you might know that your mother and I are making another go at things." The words were softened by a sparkle in his eyes that wasn't only the reflection of the car's interior light.

I still gaped. "You... What?"

He laughed. "Come inside. Before it rains again."

I let him pull me out of the car and lead me inside, wet grass smell filling the air—and a whirl of confusion filling my head.

Well crap.

Dad creaked the front door open and left it there, abandoning me quietly on the doorstep, maybe sensing I needed a minute.

I needed more than a minute. I needed a week.

Maybe a month.

Honestly, another year would have been nice.

Maybe I could just wander on back down the drive, call a taxi (which would no doubt be horrendously expensive, but—)

"Arabella!"

I winced. And not only because Mum was full-naming me.

On the other hand, roast chicken with gravy and baked potatoes with rosemary and—I inhaled deeply—was that maybe a berry pie in the oven?

Urgh.

Salivating, I kicked my damp ballet flats off on the pile by the door, closed said door against a night that was growing steadily steamier out there in the wake of the storm, and braved the lion's den.

The house hadn't changed much—at all?—in the last two-plus years. The entry hall was still lined with family portraits of the five of us, usually with me glaring at the camera, though sometimes my dad took a turn, or even my elder sister Joanne—and Mum, in one of them, though it was tucked away in a corner in the top row of pictures, practically out of sight.

The floorboard six steps in from the door still squeaked—though I had no idea why it wouldn't; if Mum hadn't had it repaired in the first ten years she'd lived in the house, it was weird to expect she would have done so in the last two years.

I sniffed, stepped out from the dimness of the entry hall into the kitchen/living room—and a squeal pierced my ears loud enough to make me wince, echoing off the dark floor tiles.

"Arie!" My baby sister threw herself at me, reminding me once again that she'd missed her calling as a linebacker in whatever football league they had for five-foot-three elfin women, and squeezed me so tight around the middle my stomach practically made contact with my larynx. "You've been dodging my calls *for six months.*"

I had. So sue me.

Still. Maybe I squeezed Lexi back. Just a little.

I did a quick survey of the room: Mum in the kitchen, dishing up plates; Dad hovering like he was helping; Lexi attached to me like a limpet; Jenson standing awkwardly by the back glass slider in an oversized hoodie that probably belonged to my dad, and BearMan lounging on the leather couch with far too much ease for my liking.

"No Joanne?" I said over Lexi's blonde hair, asking after my older sister.

Mum set the plate she was loading down on the white stone benchtop with a sharp crack and glared at me.

"Should I not have asked?" I muttered into Lexi's hair.

She giggled.

"Your *sister*," Mum said in the same tone someone else might use for, I don't know, a toilet blockage, or the clump of soapy, scummy, probably mouldy hair you pick out of the shower drain when you haven't been diligent about balling up loose hair as you wash it and just kind of let it wash down, telling yourself that it was only a few strands, how much damage could it really do, until you realise you have to clean the drain and the emergent clump is the foul consequences of your actions come back to haunt you.

Yeah. Like that. To name a random example.

I expected her to go on, of course, with the usual litany of crimes committed by the absent family member—I shivered, realising how neatly I'd filled that position for her the last two years; Lexi and Jo had better be grateful—but instead, Dad just patted her on the back and took over filling the plate Mum had put down.

Three plates, I noted, in addition to the three already full and waiting on the dining table.

I shot a poisonous glare at BearMan, someone I'd never seen before in my life and yet someone who *apparently* was on emergency Christmas Eve dinner terms with my mother.

He ignored me.

...Did they even eat human food? I knew we weren't supposed to eat theirs, but... did it work in reverse, too?

Fairies, fairy magic...

Jenson.

He stood rigidly by the back door. Too rigid. Not just 'I'm feeling uncomfortable in this house' rigid, but 'I might fall over any second' rigid.

"You said the healing was temporary," I said in BearMan's general direction, gently detaching Lexi and moving to catch Jenson in case he really did fall.

He didn't fall, did glare at me, but I glared right on back and stood shoulder-to-shoulder with him just in case.

BearMan stretched, a long, arching cat of a thing that seemed at odds with his tall, sturdy frame. "Yeah," he said. "That was only illusion magic."

Adrenalin flashed its fangs.

My hand went straight to Jenson's neck. "What do you mean? There's no wound there."

"Wound?" Lexi frowned.

BearMan gave a wry smile. "It was *good* illusion magic."

A plate slapped the kitchen bench again. "Will everyone please *sit down*."

I headed to the couch, one arm firmly around Jenson's shoulders.

"At the table."

I swerved and reoriented as Mum muttered something about animals and eating like human beings. I didn't dare comment on the irony of telling BearMan to eat like a human being as he got to his feet and ambled to the table.

Lexi sat down too, and Dad—and Mum.

"Family meeting?" I said brightly, demonstrating once again that I had zero self-preservation instinct at all.

Dad frowned at me, which was hardly fair given he was only doing it to try to appease Mum.

"Shut up, Arabella," Mum said. "Did you find one?"

I opened my mouth to ask what in the flying pink ponytails she meant—and realised she was talking to BearMan, not me. I flounced back in my seat, the wooden ladder-back too hard on my spine.

Under the line of the table, Jenson reached over and took my hand. Tightly.

My heart tremoured again: his hand was cold, clammy.

And he was starting to look a little grey in the face, too, which *could* mean he was heading toward a shift... Or it could mean he was dying.

My stomach knotted like a rope. A frayed, weathered, seasick rope that soured the savoury smell of the chicken and roast veggies on the plate in front of me.

BearMan nodded. "Jo did," he said.

Wait, what? "Jo?" I said. "Our Jo?"

Mum exhaled heavily, her shoulders loosening.

"Will someone please explain what's going on?" I'd been aiming for annoyed, frustrated perhaps; I hadn't meant to let the edge of fear creep in.

But my best friend was possibly—probably?—dying from something almost biting his neck out in the depths of the ocean during a magical storm, my supposedly separated parents were sitting shoulder-to-shoulder at the dinner table like a pair of high-school sweethearts, and we were sharing the table with a fairy.

A fairy that Mum was talking to like a normal human being.

No, strike that: like someone important. Someone with answers.

No, even that wasn't right. She was talking to him, like, like... Like a co-conspirator.

And I was sitting at the table wearing a damp bottle-green tee that was barely passing for a dress.

Abruptly, I burst into tears.

See? This. This was why I didn't go home for Christmas any more. Three-hundred-and-sixty-four days of the year, I could go perfectly fine without crying. Not a drop. Not a millilitre, not even when I slammed my thumb in the back door. (Again, a totally random example.)

But here? At Mum's house? At Christmas? Tears were practically an entry fee.

I kicked out in frustration, aiming for the table leg—and caught Lexi in the shin.

She winced.

"Sorry," I mouthed, then swiped at my cheekbones with the back of my hand.

Urgh.

I shoved a lump of potato in my mouth to give my brain something else to focus on. Damn it, the potato was perfect, crispy skinned and practically melting in the middle, salty and buttery and flecked with rosemary and making my mouth water all over again.

I hated it.

The entire family was watching me. My chewing slowed, my cheeks heated, and I put my fork down, resting it upside down on the edge of my plate as I sat back and tried to glare at every single one of them at once. Well, except Jenson.

"You remember Christmas three years ago?" Mum said with that dangerous, placid edge she got when things were about to turn bad.

I narrowed my eyes. "You mean the one you spent insulting Jenson and telling me I was an idiot for being friends with a shifter? That one?"

Her eyes sparked in response. "Yes. The one where your sister Joanne told me she'd been pregnant and had a baby and that's why Iden had left her. *That* Christmas."

If I hadn't already put my fork down, I would have done so now, firmly and with emphasis. "I'm sorry *what* now?"

Mum's smile turned poisonous. As if sensing it, Dad took her hand in his, and with his other began rubbing her back in long, slow circles.

"You thought the drama was all about you," Mum said quietly.

"I…" Well, not about me, about Jenson, but… Yes? I had?

My cheeks flushed hotter.

Jenson's hand found mine again and squeezed.

I shook my head. Swallowed away a bit of potato that had gotten stuck in my molars. Raised one shoulder to press against my flaming cheeks, the slightly damp shirt providing a little cool relief. "I don't understand."

Mum sighed. "No. You never do."

Anger washed over me, hot enough to match my cheeks. "Well if you won't tell me anything, how am I supposed to understand? I don't read minds, Mum."

"She's right, Mum." Lexi had edged to the very front of her chair, bolt upright with her elbows propped on the table, eyes bright and piercing as she stared at Mum—obviously as keen for answers as I was.

"You're best off telling them, Alice," Dad murmured, still rubbing slow circles on her back. "You know that's why you called them here."

My stomach exploded with grasshoppers. Was I going to be sick? Maybe. Possibly. I pressed one hand firmly against my belly, and squeezed Jenson's hand tight.

He squeezed back—weakly.

My pulse skipped: he was paler still. "Correct me if I'm wrong," I said to Mum with my eyes still on Jenson, who stared straight ahead, glassy-eyed, "but we are running short on time here. Can you *please* tell me what the *fuck* is going on?"

Lexi inhaled, and even I waited for Mum to tell me off—she was free to express herself as she pleased, but the rest of us were expected to mind our p's and q's.

"Time?" she said evenly.

I blinked.

"Eleven fifty-one," Dad replied, reading it off the microwave in the kitchen.

"Right." She nodded. "Good. We have nine minutes."

"Eight and a half," BearMan chimed in.

The grasshoppers in my stomach began their synchronised hopping practise. "Nine minutes until *what*?"

A long intake of breath from Mum. "Six years ago," she said, "your sister nearly died. To save her, Iden struck a bargain. It was Christmas, the time of miracles and thin boundaries between worlds, and somehow, in his desperation, he stumbled upon, or was found by, a f—" She cut the word off with a sharp look at BearMan.

"Probably found," he said mildly, ignoring her near faux pas. "Desperation is pretty easy to sense, and it provides a nice anchor for those too strong to cross over by themselves."

I frowned. Something in that did not make sense —but Mum was already continuing.

"He bargained, your sister lived."

"The price?" Lexi whispered. Her face was tight, strained—and all of a sudden I wondered if the fact that I hadn't heard from Jo in a while was maybe a Jo-thing, rather than a me-thing.

Maybe Lexi hadn't heard from either of her sisters in a while.

Guilt flipped in my stomach, sour and queasy.

"Any future child," Mum said simply.

Slippery, sour guilt hardened to dread. Any heat that had lingered in my cheeks vanished, and I was suddenly conscious of how cold it was in here compared to the humid summer night outside, how my tee-dress wasn't quite dry and the air conditioning was catching it.

I shivered. "So she got pregnant and he... left?"

A sharp nod. "We think he left to try to protect the child, maybe offer himself up instead. It didn't work. A... *person*"—the little tell-tale glance at BearMan telegraphed what she meant—"arrived to collect her as soon as she was born."

"I..." My lips were too dry. I licked them. "I have a niece?"

"Somewhere. Assuming she's still alive."

I pressed a hand flat on the wooden top of the dining table to steady myself. I had a niece. She was living with the fey. *Assuming she's still alive.*

She had to be.

"I think she is," BearMan said quietly, and it was like he'd doused me in cold, sparkling, glittering water—also known as hope. "I've found rumours, at least."

I pivoted to glare at him past Jenson. "Yeah, hold on a second, you're one of them. Why are you helping us?"

His eyes hardened, flashing the deep, angry blue of a stormy sea for just an instant before he exerted a visible effort to calm it. "It was not my Hall that took her."

"But you—" I practically bit my own tongue. Accusing him of taking *other* children would help exactly zero right now—maybe worse than zero. Jaw twitching, I straightened, pressing my spine hard against the wooden ladderback of the chair to ground me.

The tiles were cold on my feet.

That helped too.

"Baolinn is helping us," Mum said calmly. "He helped your father. While your father was... away." Her facade slipped at that last word and for a moment I gaped: Was *my mother* about to *cry*?

She got it under control almost as quickly as Bear—as Baolinn?—had though...

And realisation crashed over me like a cold wave.

"Sorry, wait: you're telling me that you guys weren't... weren't separated at all?"

My chest was going to explode. This was a dream. A nightmare. The punch at the town party had been spiked after all and I was high. Something. Anything. *Everything* made more sense than this.

"Your father," Mum said, glance slipping sideways. He smiled reassuringly, squeezing her hand, pressing her back. "Your father went... looking. For Iden. And the baby."

"*Looking*?" Lexi and I said it at the same time and both our voices sounded high-pitched and strangled.

"As in..." Lexi said.

Dad nodded, lips pressed, eyes narrowing.

I said back. "Wow. You actually...? Wow."

I knew one other person who'd been to the fairy realms and made it back successfully. Jenson had introduced me at a shifter party. They hadn't been a shifter—the way I understood it, a shifter would rather be caught dead than in the fairy realm, no matter the reason—but *one*. Singular. One other person. And I knew a *lot* of really weird people.

"*Dad*," Lexi breathed, eyes wide. "You went to the *Realms*?"

Imagine finding out your quiet, placid, go-with-the-flow don't-rock-the-boat parent had visited Mordor and come back to tell the tale.

Like, *really. Actually*.

Because although the Realms really existed, for most people, that's exactly what they were: a story, a fictional place where dreams went to die, a fantasy that made an excellent basis for books and movies (and religion). They weren't *real*, to most people. Not in the way that, say, Antarctica was.

"You didn't find them." The knot in my chest couldn't be grief; ten minutes ago, I hadn't even known I had a niece, so I couldn't possibly be grieving her.

Sure felt like it, though.

Dad shook his head and gave that not-a-smile-smile that people do when they're delivering bad news.

"And you," I said, twisting to stare Mum down. "*You let us believe the two of you had separated?*"

"I had to," she said. "It was the only way to survive."

And for an instant, I saw past her shell again, saw what it had cost her to not know, to not be able to control… And I got it. Admitting the truth would be admitting she was helpless.

I almost forgave her.

Almost.

"Okay," I said, dizzy in thought if not in actuality. "Okay. So Jo is… having trouble adjusting to being alone, or she's looking for her family, or something, and I have a niece, and you and Dad are…" I searched their eyes.

Mum nodded. "Fine, yes. We are fine."

I nodded back. "Okay good. Because this is super shocking and all and honestly no more than I should have expected from a family Christmas… But I have a man right here who just had his throat practically torn out, and a f—a *friend* who's telling me that the magical glowy fix he performed isn't going to hold long."

Right on cue, Jenson fell forward, his gravy-laden plate making a nice soft landing for his face.

Lexi squealed.

I leapt to help him, and Bear—*Baolinn*—helped me move the plate, wipe his face down with a tea-towel Mum had jumped for, and rest him down on the table with a little more dignity.

My pulse was racing.

He was so pale.

"Please tell me you can do something," I said to Baolinn, my eyes wide, my grip on Jenson's sleeve blanching white.

"Time?" Mum said sharply.

"Eleven fifty-nine," Dad replied. "Do we need to lie him down?"

Baolinn shook his head. "I'll manage."

"Wait, you're going to do something?"

"I'm going to try."

"Why didn't you try it *earlier*?"

"Hush, Arabella, let him focus," Mum said.

"I need Christmas," Baolinn muttered inexplicably.

"Now!"

On Dad's cry, Baolinn wrapped his hands around the back of Jenson's neck and began a low chant. Aquamarine light glowed from his hands. I shivered. In my mouth, a clear, cold, mineral taste, like I'd just drunk the most pure water I'd ever imagined—and the air felt damp, humid, but not sweaty or unpleasant. Like... like being underwater. Swimming. Floating, free from gravity and weight, free from intrusion, water crystal clear and icy cold and pure, unimaginably pure...

I sucked in air like I'd resurfaced, blinking away clouded images of water droplets pooling.

The aquamarine glow had expanded to encompass Jenson.

Lexi was gripping Dad's hand, her face tight and grim.

But Dad? He was staring dreamy-eyed, as though he too were inhabiting that pure-water space my brain had just sloshed sideways into—and he was loving it.

Something chilled in my chest. Dad had been to the Realms; what had he left with?

Jenson groaned.

Never mind. I'd deal with Dad's magic addiction later. I reached for Jenson—and stopped. He was still glowing.

But he groaned again, rolled his neck on the table, inhaled deeply—and sat up. Slowly, a movement full of effort, stiff and halting... But his face had regained its colour, and he was stiff like waking up after a long and awkward nap, not stiff like he was in pain.

He rolled his neck again. Winced as something popped. Shook it out.

The glow faded.

Baolinn slumped back in his chair. "It's done," he gasped.

Mum stood, the legs of her chair screeping against the tiles, and fetched a glass of water from the kitchen, setting it down in front of Baolinn with a solid little *plunk*.

I clutched at Jenson's hand. Ran my thumb over his knuckles. Over, and over, and over, and over.

No sign on his neck of injury. No sign in his eyes of pain, or fatigue, or…

I shook my head. "Why?" He frowned at me and I shook my head again. "No, not you. You." I leaned around Jen and lowered my brows at Baolinn. "Why couldn't you do that earlier?"

"I told you," he said, voice stretched, face slack as he slouched like someone who hadn't slept in weeks. "Look." He waved a hand, gesturing at himself. "I could barely do it now."

My frown deepened. "What's so special about now?"

"It's Christmas, Arie," Mum said softly.

"So?"

"A Christmas miracle," Jenson said, his frown matching mine. "I never realised that was more than just a saying."

"All sayings start somewhere." Baolinn shrugged.

Across the table, Lexi clapped in delight. "You *healed* him with the power of *Christmas*?" She giggled, reminding me forcibly of her six-year-old self; suddenly ten years seemed like nothing.

"No." Baolinn shook his head. "Christmas *helped*. It boosts the power. I needed that. But you also need magic of a kind that can work with mortal bodies—water, in my case, which is lucky since you're all sloshing skinbags of liquid at the best of times—and faith."

"Faith?" My eyebrows were going to be permanently stuck if I drew them in any tighter. "What... But who...?" I skimmed the table membership. "*What?*"

It was Dad who smiled knowingly. "For this kind of working," he said, "the faith has to be utterly unshakeable. It's not enough to just believe that Baolinn could heal Jenson. He also needed someone here who *knew* it, the kind of belief you only get through experience."

Oh.

Oh wow, okay.

Wow.

"So," I said slowly, "because you've been to the Realms..."

"Wait, you've been to the Realms?" Jen interrupted.

I patted his arm. "I'll fill you in in a sec." Poor thing. Did he remember anything beyond going down to the beach? Never mind. I'd check in with him later. In private. "So because you've been to the Realms," I said, pointing at Dad, "you had the kind of faith he"—I pointed at Baolinn—"needed to fix him"—my finger pivoted to Jen—"but only *now*, because it's Christmas." I pointed at Mum for that last, if only not to leave her out.

"Yes." Baolinn's affirmation was met with general nodding around the table.

I sat back. "Wow."

"Also." Lexi was grinning. "You didn't point to me. I'm the reason Baolinn was down at the beach with you in the first place."

"Oh?"

"You still have 'find my family phone' on for me."

My lips puckered. Let her believe that was a happy accident. I could see the triumph it gave her. No point taking that away. "So?" I said. "That doesn't explain why you'd send a f—a *friend* to find me."

Mum swivelled to pin Lexi with suspicion. "That's a good point, actually. I thought it was just coincidence that Baolinn was in the area. You're telling me it wasn't?"

Lexi squirmed, red flushing her cheeks as she shot tiny glances at Mum and at Dad. "I, uh… I, um, heard from Jo this week." She twisted around like it was taking everything she had to stay put.

"You heard from Jo." Mum's tone could have sliced diamonds.

Lexi nodded.

Hooo boy. At least it wasn't me Mum was looking at like that.

"I didn't know about… about the baby, but I know she's been, um, involved with the, with your people." Lexi nodded at Baolinn. "And sometimes she, uh, I don't know…"—her cheeks flushed crimson as she squirmed in her seat—"...tells me things. Warnings. When something big and bad might be around. Occasionally. She told me to make sure I stayed away from the beach this week."

A hard ask, given Lexi was practically part fish.

...In the strictly human-idiom sense. Mermaids weren't real.

That I knew of.

I blinked.

Honestly, right now nothing would surprise me.

"I was stalking Arie's phone, since I knew..." She shot me a guilty-looking glance. "I knew she wouldn't be home for Christmas"—wow, okay, that stabbed like a hot butterknife, and not because she was wrong—"so I wanted to, you know, feel like I was keeping her company"—my face flushed hot, probably matching Lexi's for colour—"and I saw her head down to the point. I figured chances were high she'd end up at the beach with Jen. I... I thought she might be in danger. That's why I told you," she said to Mum.

"You told me Arabella was in danger and I had to get hold of her urgently."

Lexi lowered her gaze to the tabletop, her fingers knotting like eels. She nodded.

"Lex," I said, "why didn't you just call me?"

"I didn't want you to know I was stalking you," she whispered. "I was afraid you'd turn find my phone off. Then I'd never be able to see you."

It was the truth, and it hurt. Good thing all I'd

had to eat so far was that one baked potato, because right now both it and the suspicious punch from the city were tango-ing to see who'd be the first to make a reappearance, and if there'd been anything else in there, I might not have been able to keep them down.

"Lex," I said quietly, waiting until she glanced up. "I'm not going to turn it off. And... And I'll try to call you more, okay?"

Hope kindled in her eyes. She nodded. "Okay."

Far out. I dragged my hand over my face. "Doesn't explain why you were down there in the first place," I muttered at Baolinn.

He rolled his eyes. "Shopping," he said, and I had no idea if it was the truth or not.

Jenson squeezed my hand.

Lexi didn't look like she was about to cry any more.

And Mum and Dad were sitting side by side, leaning against each other like they were velcroed.

Okay. So he'd been there when we needed him. Maybe there was a reason, maybe it was just part of the Christmas miracle. Maybe either way, I didn't need to know.

"I WAS ONLY TRYING TO KEEP YOU SAFER THAN YOUR sister," Mum said as she joined me on the bench in the backyard, handing me a glass of sparkling water. "Merry fucking Christmas." She snorted. "I hate this time of year."

My glass froze halfway to my mouth. "I thought you loved Christmas! I thought this was your favourite holiday!"

Mum gave me a level look. "The fights and the secret-keeping and the guilt? Arie," she said, raising an eyebrow. "Please." She lifted her own glass in a salute. "I lied."

My mouth hung open like a fish.

"Careful," Dad said through the screen door as he sauntered past inside. "You'll catch flies."

I snapped my jaw shut, shook my head at Mum—and smiled as inside, Jenson lifted Lexi in one arm and threw her easily onto the couch from across the room.

He might look scrawny, but in some way that utterly belied ordinary physics, he was also a shark, and had the shifter strength to match.

I shook my head again.

Okay. So maybe dealing with family secrets hadn't been such a bad thing this time. And maybe —only *maybe*, mind you—being forced to feel my guilt for ignoring Lexi—okay, okay, and the rest of them too—was a good thing.

Maybe—*only* maybe—I could be persuaded to give up just a little of my grinchiness about the idea of family holidays—even if, apparently, Mum had been faking her enthusiasm all along.

Shrieks of laughter echoed out to the yard, Lexi

screaming delightedly like someone half her age. I pressed my lips against the rim of my glass as though it might help keep my burgeoning smile secret, the sour bubbles of the sparkling water popping gently against my lip.

But maybe—maybe—it didn't have to keep my secret.

Mum shifted on the bench next to me—and she was smiling too, right back at me, a full-glow beam I hadn't seen in... a while.

I chugged the sour fizzy water down... and spluttered as it went down the wrong way.

Mum snorted—giggled—and then we were both laughing so hard my sides hurt.

"What's so funny?" Baolinn said, head tilted quizzically as he paused by the screen door.

Mum's gaze met mine. A fresh wave of giggles crashed over us.

Baolinn shook his head and wandered off, muttering something that sounded suspiciously like, "*Humans.*"

I snorted—sighed—and straightened on the picnic bench, the cold, half-full glass between my fingertips. "Thanks," I said quietly, studying the way condensation ran down the outside of the glass. "For telling me what was going on."

Mum shrugged. "I wanted to tell you all along. It wasn't safe though."

"Yeah," I said. "I know."

Mum reached over and wrapped an arm around me, bringing with her a spiced-berry waft of her favourite seasonal perfume. "Merry Christmas," she said. "Maybe next year we can have a proper one again."

I smiled half-heartedly as I tipped my glass back and forth, its heavy bottom rocking with a satisfying sound against the wooden picnic table, the warm weight of Mum's arm over my shoulders. It seemed so implausible—my niece, Iden, they'd been missing for three years now, and the chances of them making their way home safely grew slimmer every day—but what the heck.

A real family Christmas again?

Sure. Why not. There were harder things to wish for in this life. (A million dollars and a pony—to name a *completely random* example.)

I giggled, smothered it with a swipe of my shoulder against my chin, and sighed—but this time there was a touch more contentment to the sigh. "I'd like that," I murmured.

"Yeah," Mum said. "Me too."

My smile relaxed into something more wholesome. I let go of the glass, swivelled, and gave Mum a tight hug that smelled of spiced berries and tropical shampoo.

Forget the real family Christmas. This, here, right now, was proof enough: Christmas miracles existed after all.

Turns out all it took was a little bit of faith.

About The Author

AMY LAURENS is an Australian author of fantasy and science fiction for all ages. Her fantasy novella *Bones Of The Sea*, about creepy magical bones and carnivorous mist, won the 2021 Aurealis Award for Best Fantasy Novella.

Amy has also written the award-winning portal-fantasy *Sanctuary* series about Edge, a 13-year-old girl forced to move to a small country town because of witness protection (the first book is *Where Shadows Rise*), the humorous fantasy *Kaditeos* series, following newly graduated Evil Overlord Mercury as she attempts to acquire a castle, the young adult series *Storm Foxes*, about love and magic and family in small town Australia, and a whole host of shorter works.

Amy also writes non-fiction books, often on various aspects of writing. Also dogs. Lots of dogs.

You can find out more about Amy and her books at www.AmyLaurens.com.

Read more by Amy Laurens!

Available in print and ebook
from InkprintPress.com
and all major online retailers

Trust Issues

Warm steam filled the air around Becca, faintly scented with fake apples from her shampoo. The hot water pattered down on her back, turning her skin red and, in theory, soothing away her tension. Of course, that would have been more easily facilitated had she not been in the midst of performing the contortions necessary to get her legs shaved, but she'd feel better once she was done. Probably.

Up, rinse, up, rinse; she scraped the blossom-pink razor over her pale legs, shaking it out in the main stream of the shower water at the top of each stroke. Steam billowed up in her face as she curled over her leg, warm against her cheeks and the inside of her nose.

There. Nearly done.

Honestly, the whole thing was an exercise in pointless futility. It wasn't like the wolf was going to be staring at her legs. And if he did, so what? Why did she care what he thought?

She didn't, that's what. Jaw clenching, Becca pressed shower water from her eye with the tips of her fingers.

One last stroke.

Becca inhaled sharply as the razor sliced the sensitive skin over her Achilles heel, removing a good slice of flesh and making the water run momentarily red. She grabbed at her ankle with her free hand, trying to stem the bleeding with her thumb, and nearly slipped on the wet tiles. Her elbow smacked the bottles of hair products that lined the shower's shelf—and the shelf itself—and she hopped madly, trying to regain her balance. Her weight fell against the cold glass of the shower screen—and the door screaked open, dumping her unceremoniously on the mat.

"Ow." That was going to bruise her butt.

Disgusted, Becca threw the razor back into the shower and scrambled to her feet. She reached in and turned the water off, realising as she did that her right elbow was about as tender as her butt would be in the morning. She flung her dark blonde, wet hair out of her eyes. So much for getting pretty.

Stupid date. Stupid wolf.

Red streaks on the mat caught her eye as she snagged her white towel off the rail: her heel, still dripping blood.

Bloody hell.

Literally.

She gathered her wet hair to one side, picking it off her shoulders and neck, wrapped the towel around herself, and hobbled to the vanity. Somewhere in there, lost amid cobwebbed piles of lotions, powders and unused potions, was a packet of bandaids.

Becca crouched awkwardly, stretching into the back of the cupboard that stank of bleach and toothpaste—and jumped as her sore elbow connected with something cold: a festering bottle of nail polish that was only too happy to jump off the shelf and smash on the floor, bleeding its awful browny-coral innards all over the second bath mat.

The chemical scent of the polish hit her nostrils. *Urgh. Someone remind me why I am doing this?*

Perching on the edge of the bath, Becca applied the bandaid, a giant strip wider than two of her fingers, its 'flesh' tones doing nothing to blend in with the complexion her grandmother had liked to call porcelain.

"Bloody Irish," she muttered. She smoothed the plaster down, snatched up the bloodied bathmat and took it to the laundry, then stalked back to her room to dress.

Underwear, now that was a question. Not that there was any *question* of him *seeing* her underwear. She was widowed, not desperate. Even if, just occasionally, when he turned his big stupid wolf eyes on her she lost her mind just a little bit remembering what sex had been like.

But back to the underwear, she reminded herself as she finished towelling off and used the damp towel to twist up her hair. She didn't trust him as far as she could throw him, which given she doubted she could even lift him off the ground amounted practically to not at all—but could she really bring herself to go plain black cotton on a date?

Ah, screw it. It wasn't like the dress was that fitted or anything. Comfy it was. Becca fished her favourite pair of black undies out from the crumpled mess in her top drawer, donned a sensible—if slightly uplifting—bra, and from the very back of her other top drawer snatched out an old, dusty satin pencil case, the magenta one with the floral embroidery.

Despite nearly stabbing herself in the eye with mascara she hadn't applied in years, and overdoing it with the big round hairbrush and the hairdryer so it looked like she was wearing a 1960s wig for a few minutes until she managed to devolumise things a bit, Becca managed to finish getting ready with a relative minimum of fuss.

She slipped into her little black dress—always go with a classic on the first date, she'd decided; she still wasn't actually sure whether she wanted to impress the wolf or scare him away—slipped her phone, driver's licence and bank card into the cunningly placed pocket, straightened the short sleeves, and squished into a pair of heels that were dangerously tall and stunningly gorgeous: black satin with red and gold oriental designs brocaded into the fabric, nearly six inches high.

She wobbled for the first few steps before remembering how to balance right in them: Weight on the toes, pretend the shoes aren't really there, just tip-toe along with your calves tight and your core strong.

You got this.

She caught sight of her reflection in her dresser mirror and sighed, confidence deflating. It had been so long since she'd done this. She'd been married to that two-faced jerk Nick for nearly three years, but they'd dated for another four or five before that.

She hadn't first-dated since she was what, eighteen? Nineteen?

Becca ran a hand over her forehead and exhaled. Nick was gone now. He might have stolen eight years of her life and literally any chance she ever had at having children of her own—the familiar flutter of regret and longing trembled through her stomach—but he was gone.

And the wolf was safe, at least inasmuch as he wouldn't lie to her upfront like Nick had.

Probably.

Maybe.

She hoped.

Really, there was no way to know. And trust wasn't exactly her specialty, when she was used to being able to detect lies and secrets right there in the head of anybody around her.

Urgh. Why, why am I doing this? This is such a bad idea.

As if on cue, her phone buzzed.

A message from her sister Clare: *I know he's picking you up in fifteen minutes, which means you're moping around wondering why you let me bully you into this, so I'm reminding you of our little bargain. Besides. He's gorgeous. It'll be good for you.*

Becca's lips quirked into a half smile. Her sister knew her all too well—hence the bargain, whereby Becca would be subjected to an endless stream of potential suitors every time she visited Clare if she didn't agree to a date with the wolf. And simply avoiding Clare's house wouldn't have worked; Clare would have just hauled the suitors to her.

A knock sounded at the door.

Adrenalin leapt through Becca's stomach and she bolted upright, stuffing her phone back into her pocket, then heading to the door.

"I'm sorry," Wolf-boy said as she opened it. "I know it's not fashionable to be early, but the traffic was better than I'd planned."

He'd left his longish hair down, a perfectly-styled tangle of honey-brown waves that screamed to be touched, and although he was wearing a dark suit, he'd left his baby-blue shirt open at the neck, and the combination did little to hide the sheer breadth and power of his shoulders.

His golden eyes drilled through her, soft and amused and completely, utterly focused on her.

Becca realised she was staring and closed her mouth, working the inside of her lower lip between her teeth.

So the wolf scrubbed up well. That changed nothing. She'd known since she'd met him that he was sex-on-legs. That, she'd learned the hard way, was not even *close* to the top ten most important things in a relationship. "It's okay," she said. "I'm ready."

She stepped out the door, forcing him to step aside for her, and locked up the house. "Ready?" The smile she gave him was too bright, brittle like it might crack any moment, and she tried to relax.

He studied her carefully for just an instant too long, but nodded. "Sure, let's go."

The drive to the restaurant was more silent than a morgue. *And I should know,* Becca added to herself, recalling the day she'd met the wolf-boy, when she'd been working a case as a consultant for her police buddy Karlie.

The silence didn't seem to bother him—*nothing* seemed to bother him—but by the time they pulled into the restaurant's carpark, Becca felt like electricity might start sparking from her fingers at any second.

With a sudden jolt of panic, she glanced down at her own chest, relieved to see nothing but her normal pale skin. Phew. Wouldn't do to have those come out tonight. The blood tattoos had been dormant since Nick had—since Nick had *died,* but knowing him they'd be keyed to activate at the worst possible time. She shuddered and pressed a hand to her belly, swallowing down the nausea that the memories still dredged up.

"You okay?" Wolf-boy's voice was quiet and matter-of-fact, like he knew exactly what she'd been thinking about.

Damn him, he probably did.

She hated this whole inability-to-read-his-secrets thing. This wasn't how it was supposed to go. Secret breaking was supposed to make people more trustworthy for her, not less.

And yet Nick, the little voice in the back of her head told her.

Shut up, she told it fiercely.

So one person had figured out a way around her magical ability to read other people's secrets. Didn't mean anyone else knew that. Aloud, she added, "I'm fine."

The wolfiness in his expression increased a little.

"Stop it," Becca snapped. "I told you: I'm fine."

His lips twitched. "I can see that."

Lacking a sufficiently cutting reply, Becca flung the passenger door open, clambered out with only the smallest of inelegant wobbles, and slammed the door.

Wolf-boy rounded the car to meet her and offered her his arm.

Becca pointedly ignored it and stared up at the restaurant. "What even is this place?" Gaudy yellow and red signs declared it to be the Toro Gritando, cobwebs and cracked finishings declared it to be somewhat past its use-by date, and the noise and music streaming out of it declared it to be probably cheesy but definitely busy.

Becca sighed. Busy was a good sign, at least.

He shrugged placidly. "I like it."

Becca rolled her eyes. "Obviously, genius." She headed for the door, aiming for a stride but in reality ending up closer to a totter. Damn the six-inch heels. She should have known she was too out of practice.

"Hey." Wolf-boy caught up with her easily. "I know this wasn't exactly your first choice of Saturday night entertainment, but how about we at least try to keep this civil?"

She shot him a corner-of-the-eye look, and softened. After all, it wasn't his fault this was difficult.

Keep reading! Head to
inkprintpress.com/amylaurens/
secretbreaker/trustissues/
to buy your copy now!